SO-CFZ-952

25¢

CLEO'S COLOR BOOK

Caroline Mockford

Barefoot Books
Celebrating Art and Story

Cleo is looking at
colors today.

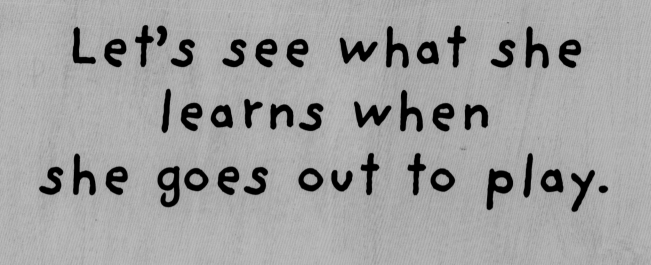

Let's see what she
learns when
she goes out to play.

Here is a bicycle,
shiny and red.

Here is a flower with a round yellow head.

Here are some plums,

all
purple
and sweet.

And here's some pink ice cream, delicious to eat!

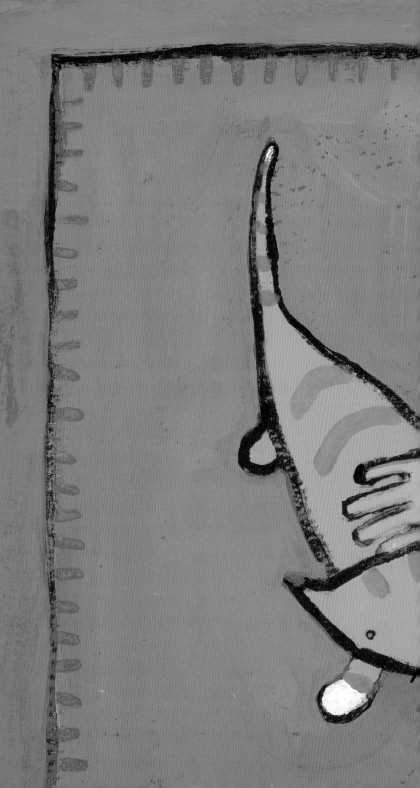

Here's a small dog
with a big orange ball.

And here's a
black kitten on
my garden wall.

Here are some apples, all crunchy and green.

And here is a bath
and a
blue submarine.

Here is a bear,
all cuddly and brown.

And here's the white moon shining over the town.

There are so many colors

that Cleo can see.

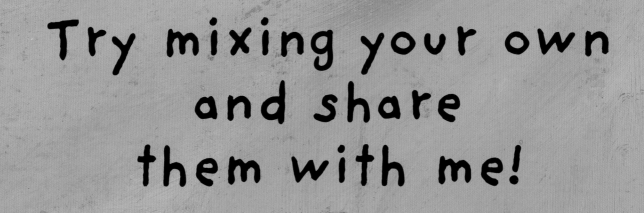

Try mixing your own
and share
them with me!

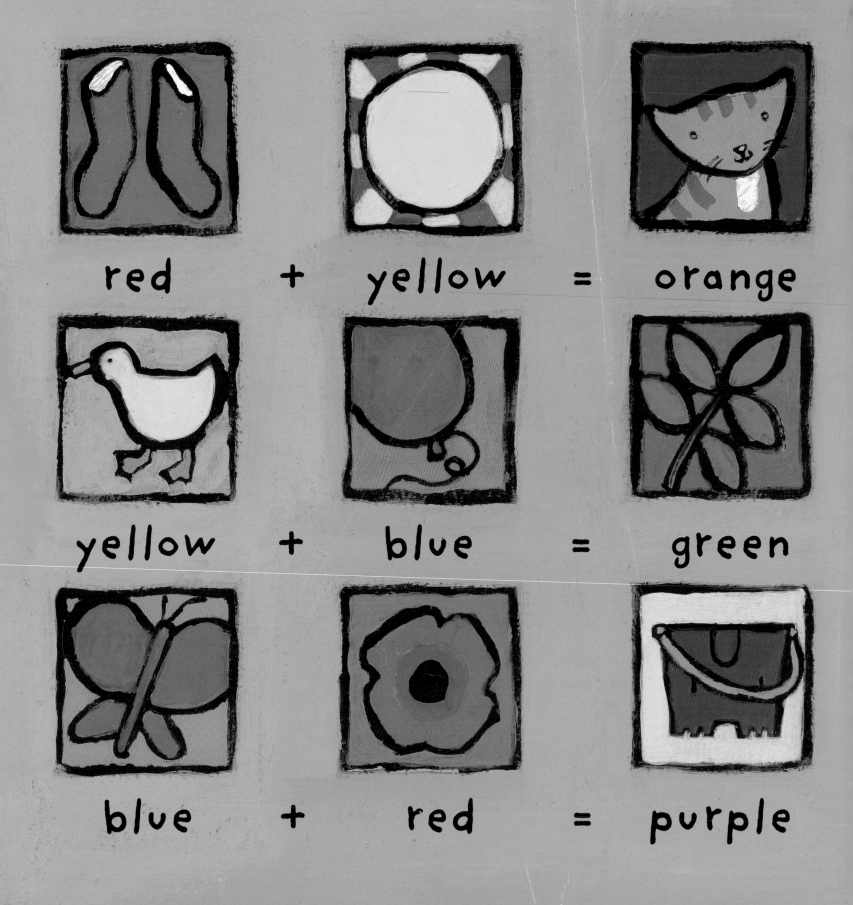

red + yellow = orange

yellow + blue = green

blue + red = purple

purple   +   yellow   =   brown

red   +   white   =   pink

blue   +   green   =   turquoise

For Jemima — S. B.
For Reuben — C. M.

Barefoot Books
2067 Massachusetts Ave
Cambridge, MA 02140

Text copyright © 2006 by Stella Blackstone
Illustrations copyright © 2006 by Caroline Mockford
The moral right of Stella Blackstone to be identified as the author and Caroline
Mockford to be identified as the illustrator of this work has been asserted

First published in the United States of America in 2006 by Barefoot Books, Inc.
This paperback edition published in 2010
All rights reserved. No part of this book may be reproduced in any form or by any
means, electronic or mechanical, including photocopying, recording, or by any information
storage and retrieval system, without permission in writing from the publisher

This book is printed on 100% acid-free paper
The illustrations were prepared in acrylics on 140lb watercolor paper
Design by Barefoot Books, Bath. Typeset in 44pt Providence Sans Bold
Color separation by B&P International Limited
Printed and bound in China

Paperback ISBN 978-1-84686-440-7

1 3 5 7 9 8 6 4 2

The Library of Congress cataloged the first hardcover edition as follows:

Blackstone, Stella.
  Cleo's color book / Stella Blackstone ; [illustrations by] Caroline Mockford.
    p. cm.
  Summary: When Cleo the cat goes out to play, she observes a variety of colors in the things around
her.
  ISBN 1-905236-30-1 (hardcover : alk. paper) [1. Color--Fiction. 2. Cats--Fiction. 3. Stories in rhyme.]
1. Mockford, Caroline, ill. II. Title.

  PZ8.3.B5735Cld 2006
  [E]--dc22